The Christmas Cave

David R. Beshears

Large Print Edition

Adapted from the screenplay
"The Christmas Cave"

Greybeard Publishing
Washington State

ISBN 978-0-9961818-0-8
(large print edition)

Greybeard Publishing
P.O. Box 480
McCleary, WA 98557-0480

The Christmas Cave

Prolog

December 27, 1960

Jenny Miller led the way down the dark tunnel. She held an oil lantern cautiously in front of her, the dull yellow glow pushing out ahead of them. Her younger brother Bill and their friend Mike followed close behind, each carrying a bulky flashlight. The light beams danced as bright sabers, slicing the air and stabbing at the rock walls of the tunnel.

They had been exploring these tunnels for months, spending most weekends here in the dark, ever since Jenny's thirteenth birthday party and they heard those stories of that kid from decades earlier.

Jenny had brown hair braided in long, loose pigtails, wore blue jeans with the cuffs folded up, a flannel shirt and light jacket. Her brother Bill, twelve years old, dressed similar to his older sister: blue jeans and flannel shirt, his brown hair trimmed short.

Their friend Mike was fourteen years old. He was a tall, lanky black kid, dressed in dark jeans and light-colored jacket.

Jenny came to a sudden halt, forcing the others to come up short behind her.

"What is it, Jen?" asked Mike.

Jenny held up a hand for quiet. She listened intently.

Bill pushed up beside his sister, looked sharply down the tunnel.

"Is this it?" asked Bill, a harsh whisper.

"Shhh!" Jenny hissed. "Quiet, Bill."

They listened. There was only silence.

"I don't hear anything," said Bill.

"Me neither," said Mike.

Jenny studied the tunnel ahead of them.

Something...

She turned down her lantern until there was only a tiny pilot of flame.

"Turn those off," she mumbled.

Bill and Mike turned off their flashlights. The little flicker of light from the lantern wasn't even enough to show their faces.

There were only the dark silhouettes of their bodies in the tunnel.

And the sound... the whisper of a breeze...

Very faint then, from beyond a bend in the tunnel: a shimmering light, blue and red and yellow.

"Mike?" Jenny asked over her shoulder.

"I see it."

"That's it," said Bill. "We found it."

He started forward, moving quickly past his sister. She reached out and took hold of his arm, pulling him to a stop.

"Oh, no you don't, little brother."

"What?"

"We go together," she stated.

"Then come on." Bill pulled free and started forward.

Jenny turned up the lantern, a frustrated big-sisterly look on her face. She stalked after him, Mike beside her.

"Bill," she hissed. "Don't you get lost."

Her brother disappeared around the bend in the tunnel.

Chapter One

Present Day

A late-model sedan, nice but not extravagant, traveled alone along the winding two-lane mountain highway. The trees covering the rolling hills on either side were a mix of evergreen and deciduous, most of those having lost their leaves several months earlier. The sky overhead was clear and bright.

Mom and Dad sat in the front seat, Dad behind the wheel. Tom and Olivia Harper were typical middle-class parents from a typical middle-class environment back home. They were dressed casual and comfortable, ready for Christmas vacation.

Jack, thirteen, and his twelve-year-old sister Amanda were in the back seat, Jack eyeing his smart phone in frustration. He was a typical suburban kid just entering his teens; all arms and legs, bushy, sandy-colored hair.

He had the look of a boy unaccustomed to mountains and streams and trees beyond the occasional family camping trip, whereas kid sister Amanda, while from that same suburban neighborhood back home, looked as though she might be a bit more comfortable out in the woods; tomboyish, and with her blonde hair cut short to keep it out of the way.

Jack frowned and stuffed his cell phone into the side pocket of his light jacket.

"Still nothin'," he grumbled.

Dad glanced once in his rearview mirror. "Sorry about that, Jack," he said. "It'll probably come and go up here." He didn't know where there might be towers up here. The last time he had been here, there hadn't been a single one.

Mom gave a sympathetic smile, but she was inwardly pleased that Jack might not be able to spend the next two weeks hovered over his smart phone.

Amanda was watching the scene passing her window, Jack his own window. Neither looked all that upset about their situation, but neither appeared particularly excited either. They'd spend the holiday at their grandmother's, and that was fine with them.

"Anything to do up there?" asked Jack, still looking out his window.

"Sure," said Dad. "Lots of things."

Mom shifted position. "Just remember, Jack... we're here to spend Christmas with your grandmother. You be nice. You behave yourself."

"They'll be fine, Liv," said Dad. A strange look on his face then. "You know my mother. It's not her we need to worry about. Or the kids." A hint of ominous overtone. "It's us."

"I suppose you're right," Olivia smiled, but the smile faded. "I wish we could spend more time with her." *The kids are missing so much,* she thought.

"She'll never move off the mountain, and as much as I'd like, there's no way we can move up here."

"I know," Olivia sighed. She admired the passing scenery for a few moments. "I can't believe... so many years. The kids were just babies the last time we were up here."

"I know. And now..." His words trailed off. He couldn't finish the thought.

"It'll be all right, Tom," his wife stated. "I'm sure it will."

In the back seat, Jack had his cell phone in hand yet again. He frowned, yet again, and put the phone back in his pocket. He spoke to the back of his dad's head.

"Like what?" he asked.

"What, like what?" asked Dad.

"What is there to do?"

"Ah," said Dad, glad of the opportunity to redirect his thoughts. "There's fishing, swimming, hiking. And you know, I think the Madsen's have a son just about your age."

Amanda piped up for the first time. 'Will there be snow?"

"Could be," said Dad. "We're too low in elevation to catch much of the heavy stuff, but I remember snow most Christmas mornings."

"Cool." Amanda turned her attention back out her window.

Dad grew nostalgic, the look on his face much more pleasant than a few moments before. Olivia smiled warmly at her husband.

Tom glanced over at his wife, gave her a warm smile in return.

"I do miss this place," he said.

§

Jenny Harper stood waiting on the porch of large mountain cabin. Now in her sixties, she was a handsome woman, her hair gray-streaked and pulled back in a long ponytail. She dressed in jeans and a comfortable flannel shirt. There was a gleam in her eye, a smile on her face. She was smart, quick-witted, strong willed and independent, all of which showed in her free-spirited manner.

The entire front of her house was fronted with a covered deck. The open area before her was dirt and grass, with the occasional shrub, and beyond stood the barn and several smaller outbuildings. Forested hills encircled her property.

The sedan pulled into the yard. She took the top step down from the porch, put her hands on her hips and waited for the family to start climbing out of the car.

"There ya' are," she said. "How was your trip?"

Tom started across the yard as Jenny took the rest of the steps down from the porch.

"Hey, Mom." They met at the foot of the steps and hugged. "Took about five hours. Not too bad. Traffic was light most of the way."

Olivia reached them then, more hugs.

"How are you feeling, Mom?" she asked. Olivia had thought of Jenny as a second mom since the day she and Tom first started dating.

"I feel fine," said Jenny. "Really. Just fine."

The kids were out of the car and standing halfway between car and cabin. Jenny put her hands on hips once again and grinned. "My, my," she said.

"Grown a bit, haven't they?" Tom observed.

Jenny's grin broadened and she called out to the children. "Well, come over here, you two!"

Jack and Amanda trudged over. Jenny reached out and pulled them both in close.

"Hey, Grandma," they both mumbled in unison.

"Oh, my." She held them out at arm's length. "The last time I saw you two, you couldn't a' been more'n a foot tall."

"Oh, Grandma," Jack groaned.

"You say that every single time," said Amanda.

"Do I really?" Jenny gave them each a pat on the shoulder, indicated the surrounding hills. "So waddya think of the old homestead? Your dad grew up here, ya' know. He spent his days out there. Not in front of a television."

"I love it," said Amanda.

"Me, too," said Jack.

Jenny gave them a wary eye. "Good answer. Bright children."

Olivia had to snicker. "Oh, they're going to love it here, Jenny."

"Hmm." Jenny eyed their clothes, their footwear. "I hope they brought along some decent hiking shoes."

Tom had made his way back to the car.

"I made sure of that, Mom." He opened the trunk, began pulling out travel bags and suitcases. "Okay, guys. Let's get this stuff inside."

Jenny turned Jack and Amanda about and all three worked their way back to the car, Olivia following closely behind them.

Moments later Jenny led the way into the house carrying a basket of peaches. "These look wonderful," she said, setting the basket on the table. "They must have been hard to find, this time of year."

"You know how Tom is about his peach cobbler," said Olivia. She set a travel bag onto a wing chair.

Jack set his own travel bag next to his mom's, then pulled his cell phone out and anxiously sought a signal.

"Might as well turn that thing off, Jack," said Jenny. "No signal within five miles of here."

Tom looked nostalgically around the room. It was a large room with living and dining areas, walls and furniture of heavy woods, a large fireplace, thick curtains pulled open and revealing large windows.

"Man, I sure miss this place."

"Whose fault, boy?"

"Yes, Mom." He nodded then at the couch. "I see you finally replaced the old couch."

"Last Spring. I thought I mentioned it."

"You did, Mom," Olivia said apologetically. "And you sent us pictures of the new one."

"Oh, that's right," Tom said sheepishly. He picked up the two bags he had carried in. "Think I'll unpack." He motioned to the children. "You two, end of the hall."

"Jack on the left, Amanda on the right," said Jenny.

Once Tom and the kids had disappeared down the hall, Olivia joined Jenny at the table, pulled out one of the chairs and sat down.

"You sure you're up to this, Mom? We're a handful."

"Absolutely," said Jenny. "You stop worrying."

"Like that's going to happen."

"At least keep the worrying to yourself," said Jenny. "I don't want to hear it. This is going to be a wonderful Christmas. Let's not spoil it."

"You're absolutely right." Olivia reached out and placed a hand comfortingly on Jenny's arm. She missed Jenny. Long conversations on the phone weren't enough. It wasn't the same.

Amanda pulled a pair of pants from her travel bag and took them to the dresser. Her bedroom was small, with just enough room for the twin bed, the dresser, and a desk under the window; but it was also bright and cheery.

Jack came through the door and plopped himself onto the bed, looking dejectedly at his cell phone.

"Poor Jack," said Amanda, and she pulled her bag over. "Looks like we'll have to be a family. You know, like, talk to each other?"

Jack slid back until he was against the headboard.

"I can live with that; for very short periods."

"Uh, huh." Amanda looked over at the window. The forest was visible through the glass. "I think we're going to have a great Christmas. Grandma looks good, considering."

"Yep. She does."

"Better than I expected."

Jack gave a heavy shrug. "Probably a home turf thing."

"What?"

"Home turf," said Jack. "Home territory. Like Dad says, Grandma doesn't like to leave the mountain."

Amanda drifted over to the desk and pulled out the chair. She sat, leaned nearer the window. The view was amazing.

Can't blame her for that, she thought.

Jack stared down at his smart phone. Nothing.

Chapter Two

After dinner, Tom and Olivia settled into chairs out on the porch, a pair of coffee cups on the small wooden table between them. The evening was warm for December, but it was still a bit cool, so both wore jackets.

Tom reached over and picked up his coffee. He glanced once through the window behind them before turning back, cup in hand. Jack and Amanda were inside, sitting at the dining table. They were playing a board game.

Jack is doing just fine, despite being disconnected from the rest of humanity...

"That was a great dinner, Liv." Tom took a sip of his coffee.

"I didn't have much to do about that."

Tom smiled. "Mom can be a bit controlling in the kitchen."

"The kitchen?" Olivia reached over and picked up her coffee, settled back into her chair, warmed her hands with the mug. "She's holding up well. She's strong."

"No scrawny brain tumor is going to beat Jenny Miller Harper."

"It'll certainly know that it's been in a fight."

That's for sure, thought Tom. *Well, we'll enjoy the holiday. Afterward, we'll take Mom down the mountain, they'll cut the thing out, and we'll have her back home before the nurses can turn on her.*

Tom had to grin at that.

Olivia saw the look on his face, and was about to ask him what was so funny, when Jenny came out of the woods, her tall hiking staff in hand. She came across the yard toward the house and stopped at the foot of the steps.

"Another wonderful evening," she stated. "A bit warm for December, really."

"It's beautiful," said Olivia. "And so peaceful. The only sounds are nature's sounds."

The sound then of the kids arguing over one of Jack's dice rolls came rolling out through the window, right on cue.

Those outside ignored it.

"You were gone a while, Mom," said Tom. "You must've gone all the way to the creek."

"I dropped in to see a friend."

A friend? thought Tom. *In the woods?*

Jenny climbed the steps, reached the porch. She turned and looked out at the surrounding hills. Her mountain. The sounds of the game going on inside continued to reach out onto the porch. It somehow made the evening all the more pleasant.

"I think I'll see if the kids are up to a game of cards," she said suddenly.

Olivia watched her turn about and go into the house. Tom could only grin that grin again as he continued to look out at the evening shadows that were reaching in ever closer.

He took another sip of his coffee.

The morning was bright and sunny, promising to be another nice day. Jenny came out onto the porch, waited for Olivia to follow her out of the house. She handed her a list.

"If they're out of buttermilk, they never keep enough on hand, get plain yogurt. But it's gotta be plain yogurt."

"Got it." Olivia put the piece of paper into her shirt pocket.

Tom came through the front door then, stepped around the women and started down the steps.

"We're going to drop in and see Carl and Emma on the way back, Mom. But we should be back by noon."

"I'll have lunch on the table," said Jenny. She called out to them then as they reached the car. "You tell Emma she still owes me three dollars."

"Yes, Ma'am." He grinned at Olivia. "Poker."

Jenny watched from the porch as Tom circled the car about in the yard and started down the dirt drive to the highway. The sound of the car faded and within moments nature crept back in. She looked warmly out at the forest-covered hills, enjoyed the morning breeze, the sunshine.

A sharp, sudden pain... she grimaced, pressed the heel of her hand to her temple.

She quickly lowered her hand at the sound of the door opening behind her.

Jack and Amanda stepped outside dressed for a hike: jeans and warm shirt, hiking shoes. Each wore a light daypack.

"Okay, Grandma," said Amanda. "We're ready."

"Let me just have a look," said Jenny. She inspected their clothes, turned them around, adjusted their packs. "Very good," she stated, quite precisely.

"Are there any wild animals?" asked Jack.

"Of course."

"Really?"

"Of course. Cougar, bear, deer, porcupine, skunk, rabbit... all manner of creature."

"Are they dangerous?" asked Amanda.

"Killer rabbits," joked Jack.

"Them and others," said Jenny. "Just don't surprise 'em. Don't be too quiet. Don't make a racket out there, but don't be sneaking around, either."

"Ma'am?"

"Ya' gotta give 'em a chance to get out of your way. And don't ever come between a mama and her babies. If you do come face to face, don't run, but don't stare 'em down; just back away."

"Okay," said Jack, more anxious than he wanted to let on.

Jenny took a compass out of her pocket. "Either of you know how to use a compass?" she asked.

"Yes, Ma'am," said Amanda. "I do."

Jenny handed the compass to her. "You stay on this side of the creek, don't cross a road," she pointed, "and keep that mountain to your south. Do that, you can't get lost."

"Got it," said Amanda.

"Off you go, then." Jenny motioned them off the porch. "Be back before noon."

They thanked Grandma as they took the steps down from the porch, started across the yard toward the trailhead between the barn and the larger of the two lesser outbuildings.

They found themselves walking along a winding, well-traveled path, the vegetation pushing in on them from either side. After a few minutes the trail turned up the hillside and grew steadily steeper. Jack and Amanda began to climb. They were glad when the trail suddenly leveled off, then opened onto a large, wide-open clearing.

They stepped to the edge of the clearing. A panoramic vista was spread out before and below them. From here they could see sweeping mountainsides of forest, open meadows, and clear blue sky.

After a few minutes rest, they started again, following the trail back into the trees. Another twenty minutes and they could hear the placid sound of water coursing over rock. They came up to a creek, followed the bank without crossing.

Sometime later the trail veered away from the creek, turning more directly uphill where the creek continued to flow its gentler course. They nonetheless decided to follow the path, and within a few minutes entered another clearing.

Directly ahead of them was a small cabin; rustic, some of the rough-hewn siding planks older than others, revealing that it had been patched and repaired piecemeal over the years.

A string of Christmas lights hung loose on the front eave, turned off. The bulbs were a mix of colors: green and blue and red.

The mountain rose up directly behind the clearing. Another trailhead next to the cabin led to away and continued up the hillside.

"Do you think anybody lives here?" asked Jack.

Amanda walked up the cabin, leaned up close to a window. Inside was a table and one chair, a narrow bed against a wall near a fireplace. On the other side of the fireplace was a wall of shelves with books and odds and ends. In the near corner were a sink and counter and small refrigerator.

"I think so," she said. She stepped back, noticed a switch mounted next to the front door. She reached out and flipped it up. The string of Christmas lights turned on. Several bulbs weren't working. Several others flickered a few times before remaining on.

One bulb suddenly went out.

A man's voice then, deep and not entirely friendly. "Waddya kids want?"

Mike stood just inside the trailhead beside the cabin, hiking staff in hand. He was dressed in rawhide pants and jacket, a heavy plaid shirt. A graying black man, sixty-six years old, his face several days unshaven. There was a haunted, absent gaze in his eyes. He set his small backpack onto the wooden workbench built against the side of the cabin.

Jack and Amanda took several steps back from the cabin as Mike moved around to the front.

"Sorry, mister," said Jack. "We didn't know anybody lived here."

Mike flipped the switch and the Christmas lights went out.

"You know it now." He gave the kids a careful gaze. "You belong to Jenny?"

"She's our grandma," said Amanda.

"Heard about that," Mike grunted. "You here for a couple of weeks, then. Christmas."

"That's right," Amanda stated.

"You know Grandma?" asked Jack.

"Course I know her." He looked from side to side, examining the front of his cabin as if to make sure nothing was missing or damaged. "Known her all my life."

There was a long pause. Mike eyed his uninvited company. His company shuffled nervously under the gaze.

"You two best be off," he said.

Dinner was a warm, pleasant atmosphere. The family sat around Grandma's long dining table, Jenny at one end, Tom and Olivia on one side, Jack and Amanda on the other.

"Oh, that's just Mike," said Grandma. "That's his cabin."

"Is he dangerous?" asked Olivia.

"Oh my, no. Not at all. Mike's a darling."

"He has a cabin up here?" asked Tom. "I didn't know he had moved back." He obviously knew of Mike.

"Couple of years now," said Jenny. "He bought a patch of land up near the mouth of the caves."

"Caves?" Amanda perked up. This got her attention.

"You mean the—" Olivia started.

"Yes," Jenny answered.

"What caves?" Jack asked, as curious as Amanda. *Caves?*

"There're caves up here?" asked Amanda.

Tom looked distractedly at Jenny, at Olivia, gave a quick glance to the kids. He looked back to Jenny.

"After all these years?" he asked his mother. "Is he still—"

"Yes. Yes, I'm afraid so."

There was a hint of sadness in that, and it was reflected in Tom's own expression. He turned slowly then back to the kids. "Mike is a friend of your Grandma's," he said. "They grew up together. At least till Mike's family moved away."

Jack wasn't about to let the conversation shift away from what was important.

"What caves?" he asked.

"You never told the children about the caves?" Jenny asked Tom.

"The subject never came up."

Jenny put down her fork. She leaned over her plate. "Well, it's front and center now."

"Mom," Olivia spoke thoughtfully, "I'm not so sure—"

"Oh, what's the fuss?"

"Mom..." Tom sighed.

Jenny turned her focus back to Jack and Amanda.

"I was thirteen," she said. "We had been hearing stories about a special cave for as long as any of us could remember. A secret place deep in the mountain where it was always Christmas. Of course, Mike and I didn't believe the stories, but my little brother Bill was certain there was some truth to them." She leaned an inch nearer her grandchildren and grinned slyly. "We were happy to go along with it. After all, exploring the caves was fun. It was exciting. It's a real maze in there. Those tunnels go on for miles. We explored 'em off and on for most of a year. Got lost more'n once."

"Lost?" Amanda perked up.

"Oh, we always managed to find our way out again," she said dismissively. She smiled at Tom, who frowned, a sparkle in her eye. She leaned back then, continued her story. "Two days after Christmas, nineteen hundred and sixty. We were deeper in the mountain than ever before, in a section of the caves we had never been in before. We saw a light up ahead, beyond the bend... where there should be no light. Flickering red and green and blue."

"Like Christmas," Amanda whispered.

"Just like Christmas," Jenny said softly. She grew silent. Her expression grew solemn. Tom reached a hand out and rested it comfortingly on her arm. She gave a gentle smile, patted the back of his hand.

"Bill rushed ahead of us," she continued. "I tried to stop him, but then, that was Bill."

"What happened, Grandma?" asked Amanda.

"He disappeared around the bend. About then the lights went out. Mike and I ran after him, but by the time we got there... he was gone. There was nothing there."

"Nothing?"

"Nothing. Just more tunnel. We followed it, searched for hours; ended up completely lost. Took most of a day to find our way back out."

She went thoughtfully silent again. Jack was about to ask her what happened when she started again, her voice more soft than ever before.

"A rescue party went in to search for him. But they never found him. Never found anything. Not a sign."

"What do you think happened, Grandma?" Amanda asked.

"Who's to say, sweetie. Maybe he found the Christmas Cave. I'd like to think so." She again grew quiet, and while the kids wanted to know more they could sense that now was probably not the time to pursue it.

Jack slid his chair back and stood up, gathered his plate and silverware and took them into the kitchen. Amanda followed his lead, and moments later they headed down the hall to their rooms.

When Jenny took her own dishes into the kitchen, Olivia leaned forward and rested on her elbows.

"They're going to end up in those caves, you know," she said, her voice just low enough to keep her children from overhearing. "How can they not, now that they've heard the stories?"

"Kids gotta be kids, Olivia," said Tom.

"It's dangerous."

"It's not that bad. Geez, every kid on this mountain ends up in the caves, me included. It's almost a rite of passage."

"Just... don't encourage them," said Olivia. "We're their parents. We tell them to stay out. We need to be together on this."

"Of course, Liv," Tom gave his wife a pleasant smile.

"I mean it, Tom." Olivia spoke firmly. "You were lost in there for two days."

"Day and a half. And I was eleven."

"They're not much older. And you could have died in there."

That last lay heavy in the room. They heard Jenny in the kitchen, putting leftovers into bowls and the dishes in the sink. From down the hall came Amanda's voice. It sounded like Jack should have knocked first.

"So what happened to Mike, do you think?" asked Olivia. "How did he become so obsessed?"

"I don't know." Tom shrugged. "Maybe he felt responsible." His mom had told him more than once that Bill had followed Mike everywhere.

"You don't think..." Olivia wondered, "He can't believe that Bill is still alive."

"Who's to say?" Tom wondered right back. "You heard Mom. After Bill was lost, rescue teams went over those tunnels with a fine-toothed comb. Never found a trace of him. Or of the Christmas Cave."

"Oh, but you don't think it really exists? That he actually found it?"

"No. Of course not. But Mike might."

After Bill went missing, Mike had snuck off every chance he got to go searching in the caves. The sheriff even tried boarding up the entrance, but that didn't stop him. His parents got so worried that they finally moved away, took him off the mountain.

Jenny didn't hear anything of him for fifteen years. Then he started showing up summers. He'd spend a couple of weeks on the mountain, going into the caves for days at a time.

"The poor man," said Olivia. "Searching for a lost little boy, year after year."

Jenny came out of the kitchen and settled again at the table.

"I thought Mike was married," said Tom.

"Mary passed away the winter before he moved back up here for good," said Jenny. "His son has a family of his own, lives back east somewhere. I don't think he ever hears from them." She looked up from the tabletop, to Tom, to Olivia. "It's just Mike."

"Not true," said Olivia. "He has you."

"Yes, he does." Jenny took a long, soft sigh. "He certainly does."

Chapter Three

Jack and Amanda followed the bank of the small stream, the narrow trail drifting in and out of the woods that shadowed the brook. The morning was almost as nice as the day before, perhaps a little cooler.

They came out into a meadow. A boy sat on a rise in the bank where the stream running beside the meadow widened out to form a pool. He had a fishing pole in hand, the line running into the water.

Daniel Madsen was twelve years old, had dark red hair, dark freckles on the bridge of his nose. He wore jeans, well-worn hiking shoes and a long-sleeve shirt.

He looked up at Jack and Amanda's approach but said nothing.

"Hey," said Jack, as much a 'good morning' as if he actually said good morning.

"Hey," said Daniel, indifferent to the greeting. He looked back to his fishing pole, lifted it, let the line shift in the water.

"Fishing, huh?" asked Amanda. "Catch anything?"

Daniel leaned over, lifted a chain that ran into the water, revealing two fish on the line. He lowered the fish back into the water, focused his attention again on his pole.

"You visitin' Mrs. Harper?" he asked.

"Our grandma. I'm Jack," said Jack. He pointed a thumb in Amanda's direction. "My sister."

"Amanda," said Amanda.

"Daniel. Madsen." He looked up at Jack and Amanda, shaded his eyes. "Your mom and dad came by the house to see my folks yesterday."

"Suppose so."

"Your dad grew up here, same's my dad." He turned back to the stream. "He moved to the city, I hear. That where you're from?"

"Yep," said Amanda. "So you live here. You like it?"

"Yep."

"You know Mike?" asked Jack.

"Lives in the cabin over yonder? Sure. What about him?"

"Just wondered."

"We met him yesterday," said Amanda.

Daniel looked carefully at the fishing line in the water, lifted and lowered the tip of the rod.

"Nice enough fella," he said. "Bit odd, I guess. Dad says he ain't been right in the head since he lost his friend in the caves."

"That's what I hear," said Jack.

"It was our grandma's brother that got lost," said Amanda. "They were looking for the Christmas Cave."

Daniel gave a slow, knowing nod. "Twarn't the first that got lost in there. Doubt he'll be the last."

"You been in the caves?" asked Jack.

Daniel only shrugged, stared at his fishing line.

"Have you looked for the Christmas Cave?" asked Amanda.

"I know about it. Ain't really done much searching for it."

"What'cha hear?"

"Well… supposedly, not that I believe it, mind you, but supposedly, some kid came out of the caves after being lost in there three years. Said he'd been living in a cave full a' wondrous sights and lots of bright colors. Them's his words. Said it was the Christmas Cave." Daniel gave a slow sigh. "People been lookin' for it ever since."

"But you ain't gone in?" asked Jack.

Daniel gave another shrug. "Like I said. Don't believe it." He turned an eye up to Jack. "You goin' lookin'?"

"Considerin' it."

Daniel nodded, looked back at his fishing line again, dipped his pole up and down yet again.

"Expect you should talk to Mike, then," he said.

Mike was sitting at his table, coffee cup in hand, when there came a light knock at his door.

He gave a curious look at the door. A knock on his cabin door was a rather uncommon occurrence. He had very few visitors. Only one, really. Jenny. That certainly wasn't Jenny's knock.

He stood and took the two steps to the door, opened it.

Jack, Amanda and Daniel looked up at him.

He looked tentatively apprehensively down at them.

"Yeah?" he asked.

"Hey, Mike," said Daniel.

"Daniel."

"We'd like to talk to you," said Jack.

"About what?"

"The Christmas Cave," said Amanda. "We want to talk to you about the Christmas Cave."

Mike studied Amanda for a long time, his expression giving away no emotion.

He stepped back then, motioned for the kids to come in, turned about and retreated into the cabin. He settled into his chair at the table as his guests sought places to sit down. There was only one other chair and the bed.

Daniel chose the chair, while Jack and Amanda stood before a large, hand-drawn map hanging on the wall.

"Wow," said Jack.

The map detailed a complex maze of tunnels and caverns. Quadrants and divisions reflected different sections and multiple levels.

"This is what you've been doing up here?"

"Used to come up here summers. Full time now."

"Wow," Amanda said, repeating her brother's observation.

Daniel slid back in his chair. "I told 'em that if they wanted to know about the caves, they should talk to you."

"Nothin' to know, 'cept stay out of there."

"You're not taking your own advice," Amanda observed, indicating the map.

"I got a job to do."

"To find Bill?"

"That's right."

Jack turned around and looked at Mike. He spoke as he settled onto the bed.

"After all these years?"

"That's right."

Amanda pointed to a spot on the map. "What are these?" she asked.

"Collapsed tunnels," said Mike. "Tremors bringing down the ceilings."

"Earthquakes?"

"Doesn't take much. Tunnels are hundred years old and more. Little bit o' shakin' can bring down whole sections."

"You get a lot of earthquakes up here?" asked Jack.

"Some. Now and again. You can feel 'em in there more'n out here." He looked across the room at his map. "It makes the searchin' tougher."

"But after all these years, you still haven't found it? The Christmas Cave?"

Mike gave a sharp nod in the direction of the map. "I know where it should be. I know where it was."

"Waddya mean, Mike?" asked Amanda.

Mike stood, took one long step and leaned forward. He reached out and slowly pointed to a spot on the map.

"It was right there."

"But—"

He drifted back and returned to his seat at the table. "That's where it was."

Jack stood up again, cocked his head and studied the map.

"You mean, it was there before, and it's not there now?"

"I was standing there two days ago," he stated flatly. "But it looked just like it did that day. Nothing. Just tunnel."

Amanda stepped away from map, sat down on the bed beside her brother.

"That day you and Grandma followed—"

"That's right," said Mike. "Nothing there. More tunnel. But that's where it shoulda' been."

Jack stared at the map.

He studied every feature, every line, every tunnel and cavern.

Chapter Four

Jack and Amanda sat on the top step of the front porch. Out in the yard, near the car, their mom was saying good-bye to their dad.

Grandma came out onto the porch and stood behind the kids.

"A shame," she said.

"We get it a lot," said Jack, his chin resting in his hands.

"It's his work," said Amanda. "An emergency is an emergency."

"Well, it is important," said Jenny. "His foundation helps a lot of people."

"We know," said Amanda.

Tom looked over and called out to them.

"I'll be back in a couple of days," he said. "Three days, tops."

"Don't you worry, Tom," Jenny called out. "You just do what needs doing and get back to us safe." She spoke then to Jack and Amanda. "There you go, children. We'll see your father again well before Christmas."

Down in the yard, Olivia watched Tom drive off. Once the car was gone from sight, she turned and walked slowly over to the porch.

"Are you two all right?"

"It's okay, Mom," said Jack. "Really."

"You know your father's work." She looked apologetically up at Jenny. "The foundation runs on a shoestring as it is. They can barely—"

"Don't apologize, Olivia. The work is important. No one's being deprived here." She nudged Jack from behind. "Right?"

"Nothing we can't handle," said Jack with a grin.

"Right," Jenny said firmly.

"Right," agreed Amanda.

"Right," sighed Olivia. "So, what are your plans for this afternoon?"

"Daniel is gonna show us his secret swimming spot," said Jack.

"The Madsen boy?" asked Jenny.

"They met him this morning," said Olivia.

"I heard he was coming home. I didn't realize he was already back."

"He said he lived here," said Jack.

"He does. Or he did, up until, oh, about two years ago. Carl and Emma have really been looking forward to having him back home."

"That's right," said Olivia. "The boy was ill, wasn't he? I had completely forgotten about that. He certainly looked well yesterday. And they didn't say a word."

"I'm afraid he's not well at all."

"I'm so sorry to hear that."

"What's wrong with him?" asked Amanda. Daniel hadn't looked sick to her, either.

"Leukemia, I'm afraid," said Grandma.

"Leukemia?"

"Cancer, sweetie," said Mom.

Jack turned about. "Is he gonna be all right?"

"There's nothing more they can do for him, Jack. It was decided he should spend what time is left here on the mountain, long as he's able." She looked up, out at the surrounding mountains. "I am glad to hear he's home."

Jack, Amanda and Daniel peered over the top of the ridge. Mike's cabin was visible in the clearing below. For the moment there was no movement, no sign of Mike.

Jack glanced sideways at Daniel. Other than being a bit pale, maybe a bit short of breath, Daniel didn't appear all that sick.

"There he is," said Daniel.

Jack turned back quickly and looked down at the cabin.

Mike stepped from the trail and into the clearing, wearing a knapsack and using a tall hiking staff. He walked around to the front of the cabin. He went inside.

"That's the trail he left by this morning," Daniel continued. "I'll bet ya' nickels to donuts it'll take us right to the caves."

Amanda frowned. "I told you, Daniel. We can't go into the caves."

"Why not?"

"Because our mom told us to stay out of 'em."

"Well," said Jack, "It was more of a suggestion, really."

"Jack..." Amanda frowned yet again.

"She didn't actually order us not to go into the caves. She just doesn't like the idea of the caves on general principal."

"You know what she meant, Jack."

"C'mon, Amanda. Let's at least have a look."

Amanda gave him a cool stare, then looked at Daniel. He had the hint of a soft smile, but didn't look to be forcing her one way or the other.

"I don't know," she said.

"You guys do what you want," Daniel said with a shrug. "I gotta do this."

"I thought you didn't believe in the Christmas Cave," said Amanda.

"I'm willing to consider the possibility."

Amanda figured Jack's excitement over this had infected poor Daniel.

Jack's gaze was almost pleading. She knew he wouldn't go without her. If he got into trouble over this, better to have his little sister along to share the pain.

"Just a quick look," said Jack.

Her resistance collapsed. They were both going to be grounded for a month over this.

"Maybe just a quick look around." She glanced up at the sky. "But not today. We have to get home. I am not going to be late."

"But we go first thing in the morning."

"Yeah, all right," Amanda grumbled.

Jack turned to Daniel. "We'll meet you back here, get an early start. Right?"

"Right-O."

"Okay, then." He pointed a finger at Amanda. "And no backin' out."

"I said I'd go, didn't I? Geez." She lowered her head. "Oh, I just know I'm going to regret this."

It was late afternoon before they made it back to the cabin. Jenny and Olivia were decorating the tree when they came in.

"There you are," said Mom. "Did you have a good time?"

"Yeah," Amanda shrugged.

"S'pose," said Jack.

"Did Daniel show you his secret swimming hole?"

"Yeah."

"So? How was it?"

"It was okay."

Grandma looked the two of them over with an experienced eye.

"You didn't go swimming?"

"Nah."

"It was too cold for swimming," said Amanda.

"Oh, that's too bad," said Mom.

"That's all right," said Jack. "We went exploring."

Olivia and Jenny gave each other questioning looks as Jack and Amanda disappeared down the hall.

"I wonder what they're up to?" asked Olivia.

"They're up to being kids, I expect." Jenny stiffened suddenly, pressed her fingers to her temple.

"Mom?" Olivia took a step toward Jenny. "Are you all right?"

"I'm fine, sweetie." Jenny tried to shake it off. "Just a bit of a headache."

"Maybe you should sit down."

"No, I'm fine." Jenny reached for a decoration. She had difficulty focusing, tried several times to get hold of the ornament before finally giving up.

Olivia took another step nearer and held Jenny's arm. "Jenny? Come on, Mom. Sit down."

Jenny hesitated, finally gave a brief nod. "Maybe for just a minute, then." She smiled warmly at Olivia as she sat down.

Olivia slowly sat in the chair beside her. "Mom?"

"Better." Jenny waved a dismissive hand. "Nothing, really."

"It doesn't look like nothing to me."

"I'm fine, now." She took a long, deep breath, smiled reassuringly. *Not nearly as bad as the spell I had this morning*, she thought. *Seems to be worse in the mornings.*

"Maybe we shouldn't wait. Let me call the doctor. We'll move it up."

"No, no, dear. It'll pass. Always does. Let's just enjoy the holiday. All right?"

"Mom…"

"I'm none the worse."

Olivia wasn't ready to let this go. It took her a few moments to respond. "I'm not going to let you take any chances, Jenny. If I think—"

"Of course, of course."

Olivia doesn't look at all convinced.

"Honestly, dear," said Jenny, and she gave Olivia yet another comforting smile. "See? It's passed. Now let's get back to this tree."

Jack sat on Amanda's bed with his back against the headboard. Amanda was sitting in chair by the window, holding the curtain aside with one hand, looking casually outside.

"Daniel seemed okay," she said absently. "Kinda tired, maybe."

She lowered the curtain and looked over at Jack.

"Didn't he seem okay to you?"

"He seemed fine," said Jack.

"Yeah. I thought so too. I don't think he's as bad off as they say. I mean... wouldn't he have said something?"

Jack just shrugged in response.

Amanda turned back to the window, pulled aside the curtain. "Maybe we should have asked him about it. Maybe he was waiting for us to ask him about it."

"It's his personal business," said Jack. "He wants to talk about it, he'll talk about it."

"Maybe."

"They always make it out worse than it is." Jack was way past ready to change the subject. "Waddya think we'll find in the Christmas Cave?"

"I didn't say I was going to go into the tunnels, much less that I'd go looking for the Christmas Cave."

"Sure you're going in."

"I only said I'd take a look. Nothin' about going inside."

"Well, that doesn't make any sense," said Jack. "Ya' gotta go in. What? You gonna stand outside and stare at it? Besides, it's like, ya' know, Daniel's Last Wish."

"Oh, don't you go playin' the guilt trip card on me, Jack."

"I'm just sayin'."

Amanda gave her brother a chilling glare. "That's cold."

Jack settled in more comfortably, stared up at the ceiling and grinned. His work was done.

"All right," Amanda said firmly. "I'll go to the caves with you, and we'll have a look around inside. But I'm not promising anything."

"Of course. We'll just check it out. We'll see what's what."

Mom's voice came from down the hall.

"Kids! Come out here and help with the tree."

Chapter Five

Jack, Amanda and Daniel walked stealthily past Mike's old cabin in the early morning, started up the trail they had seen Mike come out of the day before. Each had a small knapsack on their back.

The trail wound through woods, meadow and open hillside, always upward. Misty fog rolled over grassy fields and through the trees. It would take the morning sun rising higher to burn it off.

An hour from Mike's place and they stepped out into a clearing of bare ground at the base of a steep rock face. There was a crevice between two tall rocks that formed a dark opening four feet wide.

A worn path led directly to the opening.

"This must be it," said Daniel.

"It doesn't look like much," said Jack, with a hint of disappointment.

"What'd ya' expect?"

Amanda moved in closer to the cave opening. "Looks kinda' menacing, if you ask me."

Daniel shrugged out of his knapsack, set it at his feet and opened it. The others followed suit. Each brought out a flashlight.

"You sure about this?" asked Amanda, gripping her flashlight.

"I'm not makin' you guys come with me," said Daniel.

"It'll be all right, Amanda," said Jack. "If you feel uncomfortable, we'll come back out."

"I already feel uncomfortable."

"Well ya' gotta give it a chance," said Jack. "We'll just go in a ways, have a look around."

"What if we get lost?"

"We won't get lost." He tapped at his temple. "I have Mike's map right here. I'll take us right to the Christmas Cave."

"All right, then." Daniel picked up his knapsack, flicked on his flashlight. "Let's go."

Amanda let out a sigh and gave a short nod. Jack grinned, picked up his knapsack and led the way to the entrance, turning on his flashlight as he stepped through the opening.

Inside, the opening to the outside world behind them was a bright glare, ahead of them the way narrowed quickly toward a dark tunnel.

"Okay," Amanda whispered harshly. "We finished here?"

"Funny," said Jack. "What say we give it just a little bit further?"

Daniel was a little more determined. "I'm taking this as far as it goes," he said. "Wherever it takes me."

"Don't you worry, Amanda," said Jack. "It'll be fine. Home before dinner."

"You promise me, Jack."

"I promise. You say the word, we'll go home."

Amanda studied her brother's face for a long time.

"All right," she said at last, and with that Jack led the way.

They were immediately engulfed in the darkness. Light beams from their flashlights danced like sabers, stabbing into the dark, reaching feebly into the black, creating shadows of the three of them on the tunnel walls.

Olivia stood at the side table in the living room on which the phone sat, the only phone in Jenny's cabin. She had the receiver to her ear.

"Okay Tom, I'm glad to hear it," she said, then listened. "Okay. Okay, we'll be waiting for you. See you soon... I love you, too."

She hung up the phone, looked across the room at Jenny.

"He's on his way back," she told her. "He should be here tonight."

Jenny walked toward the dining table, cup of tea in hand.

"That's wonderful, dear." She sat at the table.

Olivia walked over and sat beside her. "How are you feeling, Mom?"

"All the better for the good news." She indicated her cup. "The water's hot. Would you like me to fix you some tea?"

"That's all right." Olivia stood and gave a light pat on Jenny's arm. "I'll get it."

Jack continued to lead the way through the tunnels, Amanda and Daniel following behind.

"Not to worry," Jack said over his shoulder. "This is the way."

"Uh-huh," Amanda mumbled.

Jack tapped again at his temple. "It's all in here. Like a photograph."

"Jack, I've been lost before, and this is pretty much what it looks like."

"No, no. No worries. No worries."

Daniel, bringing up the rear, was more optimistic than Amanda.

"Hey, being lost is a good sign," he said. "I'll bet you can't find the Christmas Cave without being lost."

Not the support that Jack was looking for.

"We are not lost," he insisted.

"Jack?"

"Amanda?"

"Jack, this is where I feel uncomfortable and we head back."

"I'm telling you, Amanda, this is the way. It's all good. All good."

§

Jenny and Olivia headed outside after an early lunch. Olivia went to one of the outbuildings and brought out the ladder while Jenny untangled the string of Christmas lights.

They had been working at hanging them along the rain gutter for half an hour, Olivia up on the ladder and Jenny standing below, when a car came into the yard. The Madsen parents got out.

Jenny left the foot of the ladder and started toward them as Olivia stepped down.

Carl Madsen was thirty-nine years old, medium build, hair beginning to thin. He dressed warm, ready for mountain weather. His wife Emma was a year older, thin and tired looking. She dressed as if she was from the city and only here on a visit. This, despite the fact that she had lived on the mountain most of her adult life, ever since her wedding day.

"Sorry to bother you, Jenny," said Carl.

"Don't be silly, Carl. You know you're welcome anytime."

Olivia stepped up next to Jenny. "Carl, Emma. Good to see you both again. Is there a problem?"

"Hello, Olivia," said Emma. "I don't suppose Daniel is here? Don't suppose you've seen him?"

"I believe he's with Jack and Amanda. They were going up to see Mike, then heading up the creek to some meadow or other."

"I'm sure he's all right, Emma," said Jenny. "They're just exploring."

Olivia could see very real concern on Emma's face.

"Is something wrong?" she asked.

"I'm sure it's nothing," said Carl.

"He didn't take his medicine with him," said Emma. "He's been gone all morning."

"Oh, my," said Olivia. "We expect them to be gone all day. They took sack lunches with them."

Jenny reached out and placed a hand on Carl's arm. "Would you like us to go looking for them?"

"No, it's all right. Just being overly protective. He's skipped his medicine before."

"Are you sure?" asked Olivia. "Really, we can—"

"No need. We do tend to smother him these days. And he hates the way the medicine makes him feel."

Emma smiled guiltily. "And we are constantly after him to take his medicine. It's probably why he spends so much time out there."

"Oh, I doubt the boy needs any encouragement in that regard," said Jenny. "You know I'm right, Carl. You remember these mountains when you were his age. Drawn to 'em like a magnet, you were."

"Yes, of course."

Jenny gave Carl's arm another pat, then reached over to Emma held her arm comfortingly.

"They'll be home well before dinner. Standing orders."

It was early evening before Tom made it back. He came in through the front door and set down his travel bag, smiled in Olivia's direction when she came in from the kitchen.

"Hey, Liv. Sorry I'm late. Hit some traffic."

They hugged and kissed, then Tom looked around the room. All quiet. Too quiet.

"Did I miss dinner?"

Olivia sighed. "The kids aren't home yet. I'm starting to get a bit worried."

"I'm sure they just lost track of the time, Liv. Where were they headed?"

"They said they were going to hike up the creek. Daniel is with them."

Jenny came into the living room from the kitchen. "Hello, Tom. Welcome home."

"Hey, Mom." He looked back to Olivia. "I'm sure they're all right."

"But what if they've gotten lost."

Jenny spoke out as she sat at the table. "They know the boundaries, Olivia. Tough to get lost so long as you stay in the boundaries."

"Not if they've gone into the caves, it isn't."

"There is that, of course." Jenny frowned. "Frankly, I'm more concerned that something may have happened to Daniel."

Tom looked curiously at his mother, then at Olivia.

"Carl and Emma were here earlier," said Olivia. "Daniel didn't take his medicine this morning, didn't take it with him." She folded her arms, held her elbows with her hands. "I think we should go looking for them. Don't you?"

"You say they went hiking up the creek?"

"That's what they said."

All three were quiet for several moments. Jenny finally placed the palm of one hand firmly down on the table and stood up.

"All right. Let's see if Mike has seen them. I'll get changed." She waved a hand at them. "You too, you too. Go on. You can't wander about the woods dressed like that."

The sun had set before they reached Mike's cabin. They knocked and waited, knocked again. When there was still no answer, Jenny opened the door and the others followed her in.

Inside, the room was dark. Jenny reached over to the light switch and turned on the light. Tom stepped into the kitchen area. Everything looked cold.

"He's been gone all day, at least."

"Look at this, Tom," said Olivia. She was standing before the large map on the wall. Tom took the few steps to stand beside her. Jenny spoke up behind them.

"That's his map of the caves. He's been working on it for years."

Olivia studied one specific location on the map. She pointed. "The Christmas Cave."

"He found it?" Tom asked.

Jenny stepped up beside him, spoke matter-of-factly. "He thinks so. But there was nothing there."

"Mother?"

"Mike's been there a couple of times the last few weeks." She and Mike had talked about it just the other day.

"Tom..." Olivia sounded really worried now. "What if the kids saw this?"

"Of course they've seen it." He stared hard at the map. He nodded at the location Mike had indicated. "That's where they are."

"Then I guess that's where we're going," said Jenny.

"Mom... maybe you should wait at the house. In case they show up there."

"What if they do?"

"They'll wonder where we are."

"So."

"Mom..."

"End of discussion."

Tom turned away from his mother, gave the hint of a nod and finally stepped over to the desk.

"All right," he said at last. "Give me a minute. I'll make a copy of the map."

Jenny took a last quick glance at the map before starting toward the door.

"I know the way," she said. She turned and started toward the door. She stopped then, hesitated. She reached out and grasped the door jamb. Facing away from the others, she fought back a grimace of pain.

Tom saw that something was wrong. "Mom?"

The pain slowly subsided.

"I know the way," she repeated. "Come on. Mike keeps a spare lantern in the shed."

Jack slowed and looked back at the others. The tunnel here was very narrow, was well lit by their flashlights.

Daniel appeared pale, short of breath; fatigued.

Jack stopped. "Let's take a breather."

"Good idea," said Amanda. She studied the features of this narrow stretch of tunnel. "We've been here before."

"No we haven't," Jack stated firmly.

Daniel took a deep breath, let it out. He looked forward and back, then at Amanda.

"How can you tell?"

"I can tell."

Jack was insistent. "We have <u>not</u> been here before."

Amanda shook her head sadly. "We are <u>so</u> lost."

"I'm telling you, this is the way out."

"You said before."

"And it's still true."

"But we're going down."

"We have to go down to go up."

Amanda leaned nearer Daniel, who appeared increasingly pale in the feeble light.

"Hey, you okay?" she asked.

"Sure." Daniel put on a weak smile. "Just give me a second."

Amanda turned to her brother. "Jack, we need to go back."

Jack looked at Daniel, didn't like what he saw.

"Yeah. Okay," he said. "I know the way."

Daniel shook his head sharply and pushed himself forward.

"Not going back. I'm ready. Come on."

"Amanda's right, Daniel," said Jack. "We should go back. We can try again tomorrow."

Daniel took another halting step, turned then and looked back at the others.

"No. No. You don't understand. This is it. This is my last adventure. I'm going on. No matter what." He took a moment to catch his breath. "Alone, if I have to."

Jack looked once to Amanda, turned slowly again to Daniel.

"No, man," he said. "Not alone."

Amanda surrendered to the majority, gave a grudging nod. She saw something then up ahead in the tunnel, beyond Daniel.

She grasped Jack by the arm.

"Hey..." she said, almost a whisper. "You see that?"

Jack and Daniel both looked ahead, tried to see beyond the reach of their flashlights.

"See what?" asked Jack.

Daniel slowly raised his arm and pointed.

"That." Up ahead, from beyond the bend... a faint light.

"Are we out?" asked Amanda.

"No." Daniel stated flatly. "Not out."

He turned off his flashlight. The others followed suit.

The tunnel was dark but for a colorful, flickering glow beyond the bend in the tunnel.

"Wow," Amanda whispered.

"Yeah wow," said Jack. "Come on."

They started forward, cautiously approached the bend. Beyond the bend, they came face to face with Mike, standing tall in the center of the tunnel.

He looked down at them, his lantern held up before him, a dull yellow glow.

"Oh," Amanda said curtly. "It's you."

"Yes. Me," said Mike. He looked at Daniel. "You okay, kid? You don't look so good."

"I always look this way. I don't get enough sun."

"I hear ya." Mike turned forward. "I got something better."

He turned off his lantern.

Several dozen feet ahead of them, the tunnel glowed in bright, colorful light.

Tom, Olivia and Jenny made ready to go into the caves. The sky overhead was gray and dreary. Night came fast here and it would be dark soon.

There was only one lantern between them, and Tom held it up as Jenny lit it. A hazy glow spread out across the ground. There were a number of footprints.

"They've been here, all right," said Tom.

Jenny saw larger footprints amongst those of the children.

"Mike's in there," she said.

"With them, do you think?" Olivia asked hopefully.

"I doubt very much that he would take them into the caves, but he may well have found them."

Looks like we're all headed to the same place, thought Tom.

"Are you two ready?" he asked.

"Oh, yes." Olivia gave her husband the hint of a smile. "Let's go ground some children."

Tom gave her a strong affirmative nod, then held the lantern out to his mother.

"Mom?"

Jenny took the lantern and led the way into the caves.

Chapter Six

Jenny turned down the lantern flame till there was only the lightest flicker.

"Well, I'll be," she said.

Several dozen feet ahead of them... bright, flickering light of red and blue and green.

She looked back at Tom and Olivia.

"I don't understand," she said. "It wasn't here. I swear, it wasn't here."

"Then it must come and go," said Olivia. "One day it's here, the next it's not."

Jenny looked back at the light. Tom placed an arm on his mother's shoulders. "That would explain why Mike hasn't been able to find it until now."

"After all these years. Bill." Jenny stared longingly at the shimmering colors in the tunnel ahead of them.

Tom took a moment to allow his mother to take it all in.

"After you, Mother."

"Yes," she said. "Thank you, Tom."

Jenny took a step toward the light, then another...

She stepped out of fractured, flickering light emanating from a wall of solid rock. She found herself standing on a narrow ledge forty feet up a cliff. Tom and Olivia came through the colorful, glittering portal and stood beside her.

The flickering behind them stopped.

The cavern was well lit. Phosphorus in the walls and ceiling created its own light, and the numerous other minerals reflecting the phosphorescent light created their own blue, red and green.

Bright, sparkling Christmas colors...

The cavern was hundreds of yards across. A narrow river ran from left to right, beginning midway up the cliff wall above them on their left, tumbling in a noisy falls. Reaching the cavern floor, it formed a river that ran across to an unseen outlet beneath the distant right wall.

"Oh my," said Olivia.

"Welcome to the Christmas Cave," said Jenny.

Mike climbed the steep, narrow path up a nearly vertical rock wall, the kids following close behind him. Daniel looked much healthier than he had before entering the cave.

They came out onto a wide landing. On the far side stood a shack with an open door and no roof. Mike took several more steps, enough to allow the kids to step off the path and come up onto the landing beside him.

"Hey." Jack spoke in a hushed tone. "Somebody lives here."

"Duh," said Amanda.

"Bill," said Daniel.

Amanda stepped out in front. "Who else," she said, and walked slowly toward the shack.

Bill, a slim man with gray hair and a long beard, came out of the shack. He took a single step and stopped. He wore shorts, shirt and sandals, all made of woven vegetation.

Mike placed a hand on Amanda's shoulder as he stepped past her.

"Bill?"

Bill looked taken aback at hearing his name spoken. He said nothing, remained fixed to his spot a single step from his shack.

"Bill?" Mike asked again. "Is that you? It's me. It's Mike."

Bill's gaze sharpened. He leaned his head forward, studied Mike, then ran his gaze to each of the children.

He looked back at Mike.

"Mike?" His lips quivered. His eyes teared up. He began to cry. "Mike?"

"Yeah, man. It's me."

"Oh, God. Oh, geez." He took a stumbling step forward.

"It's me, Bill." Now Mike began to cry. He blubbered as he staggered forward. "I found ya. I found ya. I knew I would. Danged if I didn't."

They reached each other, wrapped their arms around each other.

Jack, Amanda and Daniel didn't move. They couldn't move. Their eyes welled up. They worked hard at holding back the tears.

"I'd say this was a good day," said Amanda.

"Yeah," Daniel just managed to get out.

"S'pose it is," said Jack.

§

Tom, Olivia and Jenny approached the Rainbow Bridge, a V-shaped roped bridge that spanned the river, crossing to a landing on the opposite cliff wall. Hundreds of brightly colored stones were woven into the rope.

Tom appeared uneasy. He reached a hand out to the rope.

"It looks strong enough," he said.

Jenny grinned. "Ya' nervous, son?"

"I'm fine, Mother." He took a step. He looked at Olivia, then pointedly at Jenny. "You wait here until I get to the other side."

"Sure," said Jenny.

"I mean it, Mom." He started out, took it slow but steady.

He was midway across when Jenny leaned toward Olivia.

"Did Tom ever tell you about the rope bridge at Thornberry Creek?"

"I don't think so."

"Oh, you'd remember," said Jenny. "Thing stood for thirty years. Tom couldn't a been more'n six or seven years old. We were picnicking at the creek, the boy decides to cross the bridge. First time. Never crossed it before. He marches bravely out onto the bridge, we're all watching."

Jenny nodded in Tom's direction.

"He's about where he is now. Anchors pull out of the bank, bridge drops into the water."

"Oh, my. How terrible."

"Kid was as light as a small dog. Never would've imagined such a thing. I went in after him, pulled him to shore." A shadow seemed to brush across her face. "Darnedest thing..."

Tom reached the other side, turned and rested his hands on the supports.

"All right," he said. "Good and solid. Come on across."

"Thank you, son." Jenny called out. She looked side-glance at Olivia and gave her a wink and started out.

She stopped midway along the bridge, her hands grasping the hand ropes. She closed her eyes, smiled contentedly. Taking in the soothing sound and sweet smell of the river below, the aura of the enclosing cavern hovering above them.

"Mom?" Tom called out worriedly. "Mom?"

"Be quiet, dear," said Jenny, She kept her eyes closed, kept her contented smile.

Tom continued to look worried, but did as he was told. He kept quiet.

Jenny took in a calm, healthy breath, slowly opened her eyes. She looked... refreshed.

She started forward again.

Mike and Bill were alone in Bill's shack; four walls of twigs and bamboo-like stalks and hand-wound twine. There was no ceiling other than thin rope that ran from wall to wall every two feet to hold the structure together. One open arch served as the doorway.

Bill sat on a narrow cot, Mike in one of two chairs. There was a small table in one corner. The furniture was made of the same material as that of the walls.

"Interesting place you have here, Bill," said Mike.

"It's not much, but I call it home."

"I can't help but notice. Two chairs?"

"I could say I was expecting company," Bill said, smiling.

"Were you?"

"Nah. Gave up on that a long time ago."

"I am sorry," said Mike. "I tried. I've been trying my whole life."

"Hey, you're here. That's amazing."

Their conversation grew less awkward as they slowly became reacquainted.

Meantime, Jack stood on a small ledge above Bill's shack landing, looking out across the cavern. He called down to Amanda and Daniel, who stood outside the shack below.

"The river comes right out of the wall, over by where we came in." He hopped down in three short steps and came up beside them. They all looked down to the floor of the cavern. "It runs right below us, disappears under that far wall over there."

"Suppose there's fish in it?" asked Daniel.

"Maybe. Bill's been eatin' something all these years."

"You lookin' to go fishing?" asked Amanda.

Daniel looked almost eager. "Might just do that."

Something below drew Jack's attention. He leaned farther forward.

"Uh oh," he said.

"What is it?" asked Daniel.

"I think we're in trouble."

"What?" Amanda felt a tightness in her chest. "Jack?"

"It's Mom."

Chapter Seven

In the shack, Bill gazed off into the distant past.

"That was the Old Man's chair," he said quietly.

"I thought you were alone?"

"I am. Long time, now." Another moment's drift to another time. "He was here when I got here. Crazier 'n a bug, I thought at the time. He must'a been here years a'fore I showed up. Livin' here all by himself."

"Did he come through the way we did?"

"I guess so," Bill shrugged.

"Where was he from?"

"Don't know. He didn't speak English." From the expression on Bill's face, he seemed to enjoy those nostalgic moments, those journeys to the past. "I mean, after a few months we were able to understand each other, at least a little. He talked some about the village he came from, but it didn't sound nothin' like any place near the mountain."

"He came here from a different cave?" asked Mike. If the old man came in through a different portal, that could be important.

"I suppose it was a cave. We didn't talk much about outside. Mostly he talked to me about how things work, how to get food, how to make stuff."

So... what happened to him?'

"Died." Another shrug. This time, it was somehow sad. "Went to sleep one night, didn't wake up."

"Bill. I'm—"

"A long time ago. Long, long time ago."

They sat quietly then, each in his own thoughts.

Voices then, from outside the shack...

Jack, Amanda and Daniel stood looking across the landing as Tom stepped onto the ledge. Olivia and Jenny came up behind him, stepped up beside him. Seeing the children, Olivia rushed forward.

"Jack! Amanda!" She wrapped her arms around them. "Oh, my! Oh, my!"

"Hey, Mom," said Jack.

Olivia pulled away, looked over at Daniel. "Are you all right?" she asked. "Your parents are so worried."

"I'm fine, Mrs. Harper." He took a moment to endure a quick hug from Mrs. Harper. "I feel really good, actually."

"I'm so glad to hear that." She looked again at Jack and Amanda. "Oh, you two are so grounded."

Mike and Bill came out of the shack. Olivia wasn't surprised at all. She pulled the children aside, opening the view between Bill and Jenny. She smiled warmly at Jenny.

Jenny approached her long, lost brother. Bill haltingly approached his sister.

They held each other for the first time in more than fifty years.

Jack and Amanda sat on the edge of the landing, legs dangling over the side, looking out across the cavern. Behind them, Tom and Olivia walked casually across the ledge from the direction of the trailhead.

Amanda leaned forward, looked straight down below them. She could see Mike, Bill and Jenny walking along the base of the cliff far below, at the river's edge.

Jack glanced at Amanda, looked down at what Amanda was looking at.

"They're just like kids," he noted, smiling.

"They were just kids the last time they were all together," said Amanda.

Jack gave a light chuckle before turning serious. "Did you see Grandma when they first saw each other? I've never seen her cry before."

"She is one tough lady, I'm here to tell ya'."

"Heck of a reunion," said Amanda after a long time.

Behind them, Tom and Olivia continued their stroll, nearing the shack. Tom nodded in the direction of the kids.

"Just look at 'em, Liv. You'd think we were at a picnic.

"Some picnic." She let out a long breath, and there was a tremor in her words. "I was so worried."

"Yes, but we found them. And they're safe." He admired the scene around them. "And think of it. Just consider where we are."

"Consider just a little bit further, Tom." Olivia's words were cool now. Cool and precise. "We found the children. We found

Bill. And yes, we found the Christmas Cave. It is amazing. I agree. It is all so amazing."

"It sure is."

"Yes. Now, how do we get home?"

"Well…" Tom falteringly waved a hand toward the opposite side of the cave, doubt already forming in his mind. "We go out the same way we came in."

"Tom… do you really think it's going to be that simple?"

"Absolutely."

"Really. Then explain to me why Bill has been here for fifty years."

Tom curled a brow, frowned. A long moment of uncertainty hung in the air.

"I don't know," he said at last. It took him another few moments to regain some sense of composure and confidence. "But I do know this. I am having Christmas dinner in the house I grew up in. And I'm having peach cobbler for dessert."

Mike, Bill and Jenny walked slowly along the riverbank near the Rainbow Bridge. The stones woven into the rope sparkled.

Jenny took it all in; the river, the bridge, the walls and the domed ceiling.

"It's all so beautiful, Bill. I can see why that boy called it the Christmas Cave, so long ago."

"You're seeing it at its best, Jen. It'll lose some when the river dies back."

"What do you mean?"

"It only runs like this nine days a year," said Bill. "Rest of the time it's not much more than a trickle."

Mike stopped, studied the river. The others stopped and watch him. After what seemed like half a minute or more, Mike crossed his arms and frowned thoughtfully.

"What happens then?" he asked, his attention still on the river.

"The colors fade some. They don't go away, but the cave goes dim."

Jenny moved to the river's edge and knelt down. She dipped a hand into the water.

There was an immediate reaction. The water washing about her hand glittered and sparkled ever brighter. Her fingers shimmered and glowed.

She slowly lifted her hand out of the river. The water streamed off her hand and fingers. Jenny stood again, rubbed her fingertips together.

"Feels great, doesn't it?" asked Bill.

"Most curious." She curled her brow then and looked at Bill. "The cave goes dark?"

"Nah. There's enough that it's still day in here. Just loses some of the sparkle."

Mike continued to look out at the flowing water. "How much does the river go down?"

"Like I said, in a few days, it'll be a trickle." He looked up at the sparkling colors set into the walls, seemingly unconcerned. "The Old Man said the rocks in the walls react to something in the water. Minerals..." he shrugged. "Somethin'. Don't know if it's true. The Old Man got things wrong, and he had some weird superstitions."

"I expect in this he was right," said Mike. "Nine days?"

"Yep. Doesn't always start the same day each year, but always runs exactly nine days."

"How can you be so sure, Bill?" asked Jenny. "Without the sun?"

Bill grinned and brought out a pocket watch, held it up for the others to see. It was very old and very worn.

"Belonged to the Old Man," he stated with some satisfaction. "All these years, it still keeps good time."

"I see," Jenny cradled it a moment in her palm before handing it back.

"At least, I think it does." Bill put the watch away. "It could be completely wrong,

I suppose. Couldn't it? How would I know for sure?"

They continued downriver then, came upon Daniel sitting on the bank. He had a bamboo rod in hand, a line in the water. He looked relaxed, content. He glanced up once at their approach, focused again on the river before him, the line in the water.

"How's the fishing, Daniel?" asked Jenny.

"Had a few nibbles."

"That rod's always done me right," said Bill.

"Appreciate the use, Bill." Daniel lifted it a few inches, let it settle gently back into position. "Comfortable feel. Good balance."

"That it does," said Bill.

Jenny looked further downstream, to where the river met the wall far in the distance. The trail they were on would take them to an opening in the wall to the left of where the river disappeared.

"Bill? Where does that go?"

"Ah! Yes. I'll show you. Let's get the others." Bill spoke again to Daniel. "Kid, do I have a fishing hole for you. Yes I do."

Bill led the way as the entire group followed the trail along the bank of the river. Daniel had the fishing rod resting on his shoulder.

They approached the wall. Beside them, the river churned noisily as it rushed against the wall and coursed through an unseen underground waterway.

Bill led them through a narrow opening. They stepped into a cavern that was quite a bit larger than the one they had just left, and onto the shore of a large lake. Away from the beach, the walls enclosing the lake rose up from the water to a domed ceiling several hundred feet above them.

"Holy cow," said Jack.

"Yes," Bill said proudly. "Holy cow."

The shore they were standing on stretched away in both directions for forty or fifty feet, bordered on either side by forests of colorless bamboo-like plants that stood twelve feet tall.

Mike took another step closer to the lake.

"This where you get your food?" he asked.

"Mostly."

Daniel's face lit up. "Trout?"

"Not trout, but not too bad. And there are plants in there that taste okay." Bill indicated a permanent campsite established off to their left, just inside the bamboo stand. He started toward it. "Here, look at this."

There was a fire pit, a handwoven chair and a small table. Toward the back were a number of woven bins. Bill stepped over to a large stack of four-inch-thick logs made of dried, twisted paper-like material, the color of chocolate, each about a foot long.

"I make firewood from one of the plants that grows in the lake." He picked up one of the logs and handed it to Mike. "I cut the plants into strips, then twist a bunch of them together and dry 'em. They burn pretty good."

"Very nice," said Mike.

"The Old Man was makin' 'em long before I came along," Bill said with a shrug. He pointed to a different colored strip in the homemade log that Mike was holding. "This is my contribution. I put strands of this into the logs that I use to smoke the fish. It adds a real nice flavor."

Jenny admired the campsite. "It looks like you spend a lot of your time here, Bill. But then, you always did enjoy camping."

"Yeah, well, what with fishing, harvesting plants, smoking the fish, making logs, making clothes," he grinned then, "bathing..."

"You've done well for yourself, Bill," said Tom.

"Thanks. I do—"

A sudden tremor shook the ground beneath them. It set the surface of the lake to rippling. Several rocks came loose from the ceiling high above and splashed into the lake a ways off shore.

The earthquake slowly subsided.

"Wow," said Amanda.

"My words exactly," said Jack.

"Oh, my," said Olivia.

"Geez, Bill," said Jenny. "Do you get a lot of that?"

"Some," Bill said matter-of-factly. "More lately."

Mike nodded. "I used to see them in the caves now and then, but last time had to have been a year or more ago."

"Get 'em more often than that here. Especially the last couple a' years."

"Really? I never feel them at the house," said Jenny.

"Interesting," Mike said thoughtfully.

"Peculiar," said Tom.

"Yes."

"Why?" asked Olivia.

"You have to wonder where the quakes are coming from," Tom said, pondering.

"Here, I would think," said Olivia. "In the mountain."

"Mike hasn't felt a quake in the caves for a year."

It was becoming just a bit clearer to Jenny. "What makes you think the Christmas Cave is in the mountain, dear?" she asked.

"I would think that would be obvious, Mom."

"I'm sorry, but no, it isn't. Not really. Not anymore."

"The Old Man," said Amanda, realization dawning. She turned to her mom. "The Old Man didn't come here through the caves."

"Of course," said Olivia.

"Okay," Tom continued to sort it through. "But if the quakes originate in the

Christmas Cave, and then radiate out through the gateway—"

"Perhaps through every gateway," Jenny stated.

"How many do you think there are, Grandma?" asked Amanda.

"There are at least two. But there can't be many." When the others looked curiously at her, she said casually, "Well, if there were, Bill would have had a lot more company."

The others then turned to Bill.

"Nope," he said. "Nobody since the Old Man."

Chapter Eight

Tom and Olivia sat near the fire pit in the center of Bill's permanent, lakeside campsite. They were each using several artificial logs as makeshift seats. Jack and Amanda were exploring the nearby stand of bamboo, and Mike and Bill were walking along the lake shore in the distance, coming toward the camp but still a ways off.

Jenny stepped up beside Daniel, sitting at the bank of the lake, fishing rod in hand.

"It's quite pleasant here," she said.

"Yes, ma'am. Real nice."

"Healthy for the soul, I'd say."

"I suppose I'd say the same," said Daniel.

Jenny maneuvered herself about and sat down. She brushed her pants and rested her arms on her knees.

"Good to see you have a bit of your color back," she said.

"I'm feeling pretty good."

"That's good to hear. Your parents were worried about you. Rather desperate to get your medicines to you."

Daniel reached into his shirt pocket. He opened his palm to Jenny, showed her three pills. He stuffed them back into his pocket. They were from a day several weeks earlier, the last time he'd skipped his meds. He kept them on hand, just in case.

"I see," said Jenny. "You may not think you need them, but you should take them nonetheless."

"I've never felt better."

"Doctor's orders."

"I mean, I really have never, <u>ever</u> felt better."

"Yes," Jenny said hesitantly. She grew thoughtful, finally gave a nod and a knowing smile. "I know what you mean. There is something about this place. Isn't there?"

"I'm sure of it, Mrs. Harper. There's somethin' here. This place does something."

Jenny looked out at the lake, at the ceiling overhead. She leaned near Daniel.

"My boy, I have been thinking on those very same lines myself." She looked thoughtfully around them. She looked out at the lake, at the ceiling overhead. "I haven't had a spell since we got here. Not a one."

Up at the campsite behind them, Tom and Olivia watched Jenny and the boy.

"Your mother looks better than she has in a long time," said Olivia.

"Finding her brother after all these years must have been a real shot in the arm."

Jenny and Daniel stood up as Bill and Mike approached. Jenny placed a hand on Bill's arm. They were animated, even playful.

"Look at 'em, Liv," said Tom. "What better medicine? Like a Christmas miracle."

"Maybe..." Olivia was doubtful. It had to be more than just finding Bill. There had to be something else.

Jack and Amanda relaxed in a small pool that was fed by a thin rivulet of water coming from the lake. The stand of bamboo separated them from the campsite.

Jack had his shirt off, Amanda was in her undershirt.

Jack leaned back, his elbows propped up behind him on the bank.

"A fella could get used to this. I may just move here for good."

"Mom may have something to say about that," said Amanda.

Jack laid his head back and closed his eyes. There was a slight smirk on his face. "Comes to Mom, it's all in how ya' bring up the issue."

He enjoyed the moment, which slowly stretched into an uncomfortable silence.

He heard his sister then...

"Hey, Jack?"

"Yeah?" He brought his head forward and opened his eyes.

A tall, long-legged bird stood on the bank opposite. It looked a lot like a flamingo, long neck and thin, spindly legs, but its feathers were solid white.

It looked curiously down at Jack and Amanda. It turned its head and let out a soft "*raaack*?"

"Uh, hello?" mumbled Jack.

The bird let out a second "*raaack*."

"Is it talking to us?" asked Amanda.

The bird opened and closed it beak several times.

"Well..." Jack studied the bird. "It's either welcoming us to the neighborhood, or telling us to get out of its pool."

A second bird circled overhead, came in with wings spread wide. It glided down, flapped its wings several times and settled into the center of the small pool.

There was a slight splash as it adjusted its position on the pool's surface.

The bird looked from Amanda to Jack.

The first bird, standing on the bank, lifted itself into the air and dropped down into the pool beside its companion.

"Oh!" Amanda called out. "Look!"

A third bird appeared suddenly on the bank, and then another.

Within moments Jack and Amanda found themselves in the midst of a flock of six great white birds. One remained on the bank, but the others joined them in the pool.

They appeared to be friendly, and were not at all frightened by the two human strangers. They swam about the pool, relaxing, grooming, exchanging occasional beak touches with one another.

Jack relaxed.

"Like I said, I could get used to this."

"Yeah, me too," Amanda agreed. She leaned her head forward as one of the birds stretched its neck to get a better look at her.

The bird gave her another "*raaack!*"

Amanda laughed and Jack joined her.

Jenny walked up from the lake's edge to Tom and Olivia, leaving Daniel to his fishing, Mike and Bill beside the boy.

"Mike has a theory that we need to think on," she said.

"Is everything all right?" asked Olivia.

"Mike figures the access to the cave is only open for a few days each year."

"I don't understand."

"It has to do with the flow of the river. The same chemical reaction that generates the light show each year also creates the portal."

"So then, when the light show stops, the portal closes?" asked Tom.

"The —*whatever it is*—dissipates, and so the window dissipates."

"But this is good," said Olivia. "It means this isn't a one-way trip. We can go back. We can go home."

"So long as the river is flowing, the power is turned on. So long as the power is turned on, the door is open."

"But Bill has been here for decades," Tom wondered. "Wouldn't he have figured it out?"

Bill and Mike came up beside them.

"I searched that cliff hundreds of times the first few months," said Bill. "There was no way back. I assumed there was no way back."

"Makes sense," said Olivia. "And so you finally quit looking."

Jenny took her brother's arm. "For all Bill knew, it was a one-way door."

"Ah, but Mike knows something that Bill never knew." Tom looked at Mike. "You know that the way here had opened, then closed, and then opened again."

"And it only lasts a few days."

"And here, in the cave, the river only flows a few days."

While the river flows, the lights shine bright. When the river dies back, the lights dim.

"The river is flowing now," said Jenny.

At that moment, the earth began to tremble yet again, and there was a low, grumbling sound. The shaking slowly faded, the grumbling slowly faded.

Oh my, thought Olivia. *I could certainly do with a little less of that, if you please.*

She wondered aloud, "If this is true, how long do we have? How much longer is the door open?" She looked at Bill. "You said the river runs for nine days a year."

"We still have a few days," he said. "It usually runs full right up to the last, then slows to a trickle pretty quick."

"Good," said Jenny. "I think we could all do with a few hours' sleep. It's been a very long day."

Olivia looked at Jenny with some concern. She looked okay. Very good, in fact. "Are you feeling okay, Mom?"

"Wonderful, dear. Never better. But it is awfully late, and it's a long way home."

"Mom's right," said Tom. He looked at his watch. It was the middle of the night. "It's long past my bedtime, and there's a maze of tunnels to get through once we get back into the caves. I know I can do with some rest. Best we start back fresh."

"If Mike is right," said Olivia, "and there is a way home..."

"Then we find the opening before it closes for another year," said Tom.

If we miss it, we're here for another year. Worse, if Mike is wrong, and there isn't an opening, we're here forever.

But she agreed, it was very late and despite her anxiety, she was very tired. They all were. After all, it was the middle of the night.

Bill started a fire in the fire pit, and after a light meal of dried fish everyone settled in for a few hours of rest. Most thought they were too excited after the day's events and too anxious about the possibility of finding a way out to get any sleep, but in a matter of minutes all were in a deep slumber.

Ninety minutes later, the fire little more than a warm glow, there came a slowly rising rumble. The ground began to shake. It was mild at first, but gradually grew in intensity. No one woke.

Small bits of rock fell from the ceiling, splashing harmlessly into the lake.

The rumbling sound grew louder. The ground shook more violently.

The sleepers began to wake, to sit up, to look about uncertainly.

There were several great splashes out in the middle of the lake as larger chunks of rock fell from the ceiling.

Fully awake now and realizing what was happening, Tom jumped to his feet. "Everybody up!"

Amanda was in a growing panic. "Dad?"

"Up! Up!" Tom circled the group. "Let's go!"

"Let's go, sweetie." Olivia grabbed Amanda's hand. She reached out for Jack, then, and the three of them started toward the opening to the inner cave. The others followed after them, several stumbling as the quake shook the ground violently beneath them. Rocks continued to rain down from above.

They were still thirty feet from the opening out of the lake cavern when it suddenly collapsed before them, billowing out dirt and stone dust.

Olivia didn't waste a moment. She pulled her children toward the wall, hovered over them, pulled them in close and pushed them down to their knees at the base of the wall.

The others in the group followed her lead, dropping down at the foot of the wall and covering their heads to protect themselves from the storm of falling rocks.

Chapter Nine

Tom was several feet up on the pile of rubble that blocked the way out of the lake cavern, pulling at rocks that when freed rolled down the pile, gradually forming a heap at the base.

Jenny and Olivia stood about a dozen yards away and were deep in their own discussion, while the kids were walking toward the campsite.

Tom pulled at another stone and let it fall away. He clambered up another few inches and poked his head into the small opening that he had managed to create.

"It's not that bad, really. I can see the other side." He pulled at another stone. This one wouldn't give. He leaned back and looked down at the upturned faces of Jenny and his mother.

"A bit of work, but—"

"How long ya' think, Tom?" asked Jenny.

"Hard to say, but not long."

"If Mike is right," said Olivia, "and the way out is going to close when the river stops, we have until tomorrow. At the latest. And it won't open again for a year."

Jenny frowned, dark and fretful. "And I had to talk us into a night's sleep."

"No, Mom," said Olivia. "You were right. Besides, we were only asleep for an hour and a half."

"At least we'd be on the other side of that pile of rocks."

Tom worked his way down and wiped rock dust from his hands. "We'll be fine. A bit of work, like I said, but we can do it. We only need an opening large enough to crawl through."

Jenny turned away, shook her head despairingly as she walked away. Tom watched her go, started to say something but finally decided against it. He instead called to Mike and Bill to come help clear away the heap of broken rock that he had been building up at the base of the blockage.

He looked once more at the retreating figure of his mother before turning again to the wall and climbed back up to within reach of the opening he had been creating.

Olivia told him she would be back and followed after Jenny. She came up beside her as the two stood at the shore of the lake.

"Mom? Are you feeling okay?"

"I'm fine," said Jenny. She couldn't look at Olivia. She kept her gaze out across the surface of the lake.

Olivia gently placed a hand on Jenny's arm. "Whatever happens, we're going to be all right."

"I suppose."

"This isn't your fault."

"If I hadn't insisted that we rest before heading back, we'd be in the other cave, maybe even in the tunnels by now."

"Don't you worry. They'll have the way clear in no time." She spoke with more confidence than she felt, more than she herself had expressed even before the wall collapse. She was afraid. The thought of being trapped here for a whole year was terrifying. But while she was concerned that her children might have to live primitive lives while they waited, she knew they could survive it if they had to.

Unless something bad happened; like collapsing ceilings due to earthquakes.

Or illness...

"Mom, how do you feel? Honestly?"

Jenny knew what Olivia was thinking. "I feel better than I have in years, dear."

"You're not just saying that?"

"No need to worry about me," she said.

"Jenny?"

Jenny looked about them, now with mixed emotions.

"There's something here, Olivia. Something in the air, the water, something in the rocks... something."

Jack and Amanda crossed the campsite and through the bamboo stand behind it. The surface of the pool was still. There was no sign of the birds.

"I'm sure they're okay, Jack," said Amanda.

"I'm sure you're right." Jack looked up to the dome of the cavern. He looked again at the pool, behind them at the bamboo wall. "We should get back."

The flow of the river winding along the floor was down to thin rivulets, the riverbed exposed in many locations. The walls and ceiling of this smaller cavern still had the glow, the colorful crystals in the riverbed, set into the rock walls and even wound into the rope of the Rainbow Bridge glittered and sparkled.

Nonetheless, the Christmas Cave was starting to dim. Dusk was coming.

Mike's head appeared in the small opening midway up the pile of rubble that blocked the way between the Christmas Cave and the Lake Cavern. He took a moment to take in the scene.

"I'm through!" he called back behind him. He pushed his shoulders through, scrambled out of the opening and worked his way down to the floor. He straightened, wiped his pants and shirt. "Come on across."

He wandered toward the river. He didn't like the look of it.

Tom's head appeared in the opening next. He looked about him, saw Mike kneeling in the distance.

"How's it look?" he asked.

Mike spoke absently over his shoulder. "We might want to pick up the pace."

Tom looked anxiously about him as he worked his way free and scrambled down. He turned about then and helped Jenny come through.

Meanwhile, Olivia, Bill and Amanda stood waiting near the opening on the lake cavern side of the opening. Amanda looked behind her, saw Jack standing a few yards away. He was looking in the direction of the lake.

"Jack," said Amanda, approaching. "We have to go."

Jack said nothing at first. He smiled then, nodded at something out above the lake.

"Look," he said.

He could see the silhouettes of half a dozen birds gliding smoothly above the water.

Mike stood at the river's edge. Jenny and Tom came up beside him.

"We haven't much time," said Mike.

"If we're not already too late," said Jenny.

Tom noted the colorful crystals that continued to sparkle through the cavern. No, it wasn't closed just yet.

Behind them, the Jack and Amanda helped Bill struggle through and scramble down to the floor.

"Looks like the river's going down, Bill," said Jack.

"It certainly does," said Bill, looking across the floor. "It certainly does."

"How long ya' figure, then?"

"Well," Bill sighed. "I expect the lights to start dimming any time now, history holds true. As for the portal outta here... since I never knew it was there, I'm afraid I couldn't tell ya'."

"Probably fades with the lights," said Amanda.

"Reasonable," said Bill.

"Then we better not waste any time," said Jack.

Olivia's head and shoulders appeared in the opening above them. "Little help here," she said.

All three rushed to help.

"Sorry, Mom," said Jack.

"Terribly sorry, Ma'am," said Bill.

Olivia was brought through, and finally Daniel. Once everyone was back into the Christmas Cave, they gathered at the river's edge and then started upriver. As they approached the Rainbow Bridge, Daniel was the first to note the stones woven into the rope, speaking mostly to Jack and Amanda.

"Do the crystals look like they're dimming to you?"

"Maybe," said Jack. "A little."

"Could be just less sparkle coming up from the river," said Amanda.

"Maybe," said Jack.

"We'll make it," said Amanda.

Tom stood at the bridge, waved for his mother to start across. She gave a quick nod and stepped up, started across. Tom then looked over at the kids, waved them over. He lined them up, held a hand on Daniel's shoulder and waited.

Jenny reached the other side and stepped off the bridge.

"Okay, Daniel," said Tom, and started him across.

Jack and Amanda stepped up and waited their turns.

"Daniel looks better, ya' think?" asked Amanda.

"Same as always," Jack shrugged.

"You don't think he looks better?"

"I always thought he looked fine."

Amanda gave him a reproachful look. "No you didn't."

Across the river, Jenny held out a hand and Daniel took it as he stepped off the bridge.

"How are you holdin' up there, Daniel?" asked Jenny.

Daniel gave a positive nod, turned and looked back behind him. Amanda was starting across. She was moving quickly and confidently.

Daniel was worried; not that they wouldn't reach the portal out of the cavern in time, but that they would.

What will happen to me when we leave the Christmas Cave, he wondered.

Jenny glanced down at the boy, saw that something was troubling him.

"Daniel?" she prompted.

"Nothing." Daniel struggled with his words. "I just... do you think we'll get sick again?"

"I honestly don't know."

Amanda finished her journey across. She immediately turned around and looked over at Jack. He started over.

Daniel is right, she thought. *The crystals are growing dimmer.*

Jack was midway across. The ground began to shake. A deep rumbling rolled through the cavern. The shaking intensified.

Jack struggled to maintain his balance, his feet on the single bottom rope, a hand holding tight to each of the handrail ropes.

Soccer ball sized rocks fell from above, splashed into the small pools of water and struck the rocks that made up the now mostly-exposed riverbed.

Jack's feet slipped from the foot rope of the bridge. He desperately hung onto the handrails.

Olivia cried out as Tom rushed out onto the bridge.

"Hang on there, Jack!" he called. "I got ya'!"

He reached him quickly, grasped the boy under the arm with one hand while holding onto the rope rail with the other.

The earthquake faded, the world stilled.

Tom pulled Jack up and the boy regained his footing.

"Jack!" Olivia called out. She was several steps out on the bridge. "Tom!"

"He's fine, Liv. Wait there," said Tom. He turned back to Jack. "Let's get across before your mother comes out here to rescue us both."

Jack just managed to get out, "Thanks, Dad."

"No problem, kiddo," said Dad. *Really… no problem at all.*

They worked their way the rest of the way across, quickly reached the other side. Jenny stretched out a hand and pulled Jack to her.

"Oh, you gave me a fright, boy!"

On the other side of the river, Olivia had already started over. Bill and Mike stood ready to follow her.

"Sorry, Grandma," Jack mumbled.

Jenny gave him a playful smack on the shoulder, then again pulled him to her. Olivia reached them within moments, and in another minute everyone was safely across the bridge.

The group continued to work their way across the floor of the cavern and then up the steep wall to the ledge where they had first come into the Christmas Cave. Once there, none knew exactly where the portal was, or should be, but they were all certain they were in the right place.

"It has to be here," said Mike, as he rubbed his hands across the rock.

"Maybe we're too late," said Jenny.

"I don't think so," said Olivia. She indicated the cavern behind them. "We still have the colors."

"Everyone look for it," said Tom. "Spread out. Look for it."

Mike continued to mumble, almost to himself, "It has to be here... it has to be here..."

Jack, Amanda and Daniel moved apart, sidestepping as they pressed hands against the stone of the cliff wall.

"I am so sorry," said Jenny. She stepped slowly back, held her hands to her face, over her mouth, fraught with grief. "I am so, so sorry."

"What are you talking about?" said Mike, brought out of his own distressing thoughts. "It's not your fault."

"If we had left the lake sooner."

"Mother, that's nonsense," said Tom.

"If it's anybody's fault, Jen, it's mine," said Bill. "You're here because of me."

"Oh, dear Bill." Jenny grew increasingly tearful. "Don't you ever—"

"If I had listened to you. If I hadn't run ahead..."

"Oh, Bill. An excited little boy runs toward magical Christmas lights. How can that possibly—"

"Here!" Amanda suddenly cried out. "Here!"

All looked to Amanda as she pulled her hand away from the cliff wall."

"Amanda?" Olivia asked.

"I found it." She moved her hand cautiously forward. Her fingers disappeared into the rock. A flickering of bright colors surrounded her hand, then her wrist. She pulled her hand back and smiled.

"Good job, Amanda," said Tom. He wrapped an arm about Amanda's shoulders, looked over at the others in the group. "All right, everyone. Let's go."

Jack stepped forward, looked about him with a wide grin.

"See ya' on the other side," he sighed spookily. He raised his hands up before him, moved forward, and disappeared through the rock.

Bill was awestruck. "I'll be."

"Most likely," said Mike.

A faint rumbling rolled through the cavern. The earth vibrated, again quieted.

Tom looked anxiously about, motioned quickly to Olivia.

"After you," he said.

"Okay," Olivia said softly, and she stepped forward. "Don't be long."

"Right behind you, hon," Tom said as Olivia stepped through the portal. He looked around at those who remained, focused finally on Daniel. "Waddya say, Daniel? Let's go."

Daniel took a step back, not forward.

"Daniel?" Tom asked curiously.

"I don't know," said Daniel.

"It's perfectly safe."

Jenny moved up and put an arm around Daniel. "It's not that, Tom," she said.

As Tom tried to sort out what the heck was going on with his mother and Daniel, Bill turned away and looked out across the Christmas Cave.

Mike stepped up beside him. "You're not thinking of staying, are you?"

"No. Of course not." Bill let out a deep sigh. "It has been home for a very, very long time. Good and bad."

"Of course." Mike rested a comforting hand on Bill's shoulder.

Bill took a final look out at the cavern. It was continuing to dim. He nodded to the portal behind them.

"Guess we need to be getting outta here, huh?"

"Yep."

They turned in tandem and approached the portal. Bill calmly stepped through and disappeared.

Mike pointed a sharp finger at Jenny. "Don't you be foolish," he said curtly, and followed Bill.

"Mother," said Tom.

Jenny still had an arm around Daniel.

"It's all right, Tom."

"I feel good," said Daniel, pleading. "I feel real good."

The cave continued to grow darker, less enchanting.

"You can't stay here, son," said Tom. He gave his mother a severe look. "You can't stay here."

The earth rumbled. The deep grumbling grew louder. The shaking grew increasingly intense.

The cave tunnels looked dark and confining after the openness of the Christmas Cave. They were short and narrow and the only light came from a single flashlight Jack was holding, and from the portal, a faint cloud of flickering color.

The earthquake continued to grow increasingly violent here on this side as well, making the tunnel all the more claustrophobic.

Everyone was looking to the portal, waiting anxiously for Tom, Jenny and Daniel.

Olivia whispered under her breath. "Come on, come on, come on."

Daniel appeared. There was an audible sigh of relief from everyone in the tunnel.

He stepped forward, was followed a few moments later by Jenny. She turned and took a step back.

The cloud of color continued to fade. The ground continued to shake and there was the constant low rumbling noise.

Tom stepped through. Olivia rushed up to him and hugged him.

Behind him, the portal closed.

The earthquake stopped suddenly, decisively, at that exact moment; at the very second the portal closed.

A heavy silence hung in the air.

"Well," Jenny said at last, breaking the silence. "That was rather sudden."

There were a few nervous chuckles.

"Is that possible?" asked Amanda. "The earthquake is there, but not here?"

"Amanda," Jack groaned. "We just passed through a portal that leads to some place called the Christmas Cave, and you wonder what's possible?"

"Right," said Amanda. "Good point."

Tom picked up the lantern that Jenny had left in the tunnel and Mike helped him get it lit. The other flashlights were turned on and the group made ready to get the heck out of there. The earthquake may have stopped, but the caves were still very unstable.

Mike led the way, confident of the path to the surface. Jack and Amanda brought up the rear.

"Do you think Mom was serious?" Jack asked his sister.

"What? Oh, yeah. We're grounded, all right."

"For six months? I mean... hey, we found Bill."

"Mike found Bill. We just happened to be with him at the time."

"S'pose you could look at it that way," said Jack, frowning. He suddenly grinned. "But the Christmas Cave. We found the Christmas Cave."

"Sure did."

"So cool... and you wanted to turn back."

"Sure did," she said again. "And I'm still grounded. Thanks for that."

As she finished those last words, they heard a low rumbling noise coming from the tunnel behind them.

"What is that?" she asked. "Another quake?"

"No. Not a quake. Oh, geez." Jack called out then to the rest of the group ahead of them. "Cave in! Cave in!"

The tunnel ceiling was beginning to collapse behind them. Dirt and dust billowed toward them. They ran. They all ran as fast as they could, but it didn't seem that it would be fast enough.

Leading the way, Mike saw thin streams of light far up ahead. He rushed toward it, everyone right behind him. The cloud of dirt and dust engulfed Jack and Amanda, still trailing the others.

§

The sun, enveloped in a glow of dark orange and red, was just coming up above the horizon. Golden rays streaked across the treetops and filled the clearing with the morning light.

A loud rolling rumble accompanied a great cloud of dirt and dust that swelled out of the cave entrance. Mike was little more than a silhouette in the cloud as he stumbled out. Jenny staggered out after him. Mike held out a supportive hand as she stepped past him. She dropped down to one knee, then both knees, leaned forward and began coughing.

Others came staggering out, dark shadows in the expanding cloud of billowing dirt. Last out were Jack and Amanda, hacking and choking. Olivia stumbled over to them, held them in her arms.

Tom placed a hand on Daniel, absently wrapped an arm around him.

The dust settled and the air slowly cleared. Jack turned and looked back toward the hillside. The cave entrance was gone.

"That's that," he said softly.

The world grew quiet. Bill took several steps toward the edge of the clearing. He looked outward, up at the sky... out toward the horizon.

Mike stepped up beside him. Jenny joined him.

The sun rose fully up from the horizon. Bright orange light splashed across the landscape.

"Welcome home, Bill," said Mike.

Chapter Ten

Jenny was sitting at one end of her dining room table, Christmas dinner spread out before her. Good company, good food, wonderful aromas. Olivia, Jack and Amanda sat to either side of her, Tom at the far end of the table. Two dirty plates sat in front of two now-empty chairs.

Tom leaned back in his chair, gave his belly a tender pat.

"Oh, Mother, Mother, Mother. I am absolutely stuffed."

"No room for cobbler, then?" she asked, teasingly.

"Oh boy," he grumbled, thumped his belly. "Five minutes. That'll give time for dinner to settle."

"Dad! That's disgusting," said Amanda.

Tom grabbed at his belly with both hands and gave it a good shake. "There we go. Fill in those empty spaces. Still plenty of room in there."

"Ah, geez," Amanda groaned.

"Tom!" cried Olivia.

Jack laughed cheerily with his dad.

Tom belched. "Oh! Excuse me!"

Jack laughed again.

The front door opened and Mike and Bill came back into the house.

"You've done a wonder with the place, Jen," said Bill.

"Get back over here and sit down, you two," said Jenny. "Time for dessert."

"Cobbler!" Tom cried out over his shoulder. "Finest in the western hemisphere."

"Never one to pass on cobbler," said Mike, and the two of them settled into the empty chairs.

"This has gotta be just about the best Christmas ever," said Bill.

Jenny leaned back to better take in the scene of her family around the dining table.

"It most certainly is."

A nice evening out; dusk, not yet dark. Tom and Olivia came out onto the porch, stood at the top step. They were dressed warm.

Laughter spilled out from inside the house. Jenny, Mike and Bill could be seen through the window, seated around the dining table.

"I don't imagine they'll be getting much sleep tonight," said Tom. "Me, I am dog tired."

"They have a lot of years to catch up on," said Olivia.

"A lifetime."

There was another round of laughter from inside. Despite that, a hint of sadness shadowed Olivia's face.

"Alone… all those years," she said quietly.

"Yeah. Once the Old Man passed on."

"And a way out, if he'd only known it was there."

A Christmas present, thought Tom. *Every year, just waiting to be unwrapped.*

It began to snow. It fell lightly at first, then the flakes grew larger, more numerous. The string of Christmas lights running along the rain gutter turned on, sending red and green and blue light out across the yard.

"A white Christmas after all," said Tom. He lifted an arm and Olivia slipped under it. They snuggled up close and watched the snowfall. The Christmas card setting was interrupted finally by the sound of an approaching vehicle. The Madsen vehicle came up into the yard and pulled up in front of the house.

Daniel and his parents climbed out of the car.

"Daniel, my boy," said Tom.

"Hey, Mr. Harper."

"Merry Christmas," said Olivia.

"Merry Christmas, you two," said Emma.

Tom took the steps down to the yard. "And a fine one it is, Emma, Carl."

Olivia followed him down from the porch and they all hugged and exchanged greetings all over again. Daniel's parents were happy and cheery. All the past worries and concerns had clearly washed away.

Tom started back up the steps, motioned the others to follow.

"Glad you could join us, Carl," he said. "Say... do you like cobbler? Of course you do. Silly question."

§

Jack came into Amanda's room, hopped onto her bed and slid back against the headboard. Amanda was sitting at her desk, the curtains of the window pulled aside. Outside, snow was falling.

Jack frowned at his smart phone, tossed it on the bed beside him.

Amanda glanced in his direction, smirked. "Why do you keep bothering with that?"

"No reason. It's just my only connection to the real world, is all."

"Real world?"

"Yeah. Real world."

"How can the real world possibly compete with what we've been through?"

"Can't," he said matter-of-factly. "Doesn't mean it isn't there. Doesn't mean we don't have to go back to it. It's where we live."

"Well, that's depressing."

Daniel came in through the open door. "Not necessarily," he said. He sat on the edge of the bed.

"Hey, dude," said Jack.

"Waddya mean, not necessarily?" asked Amanda.

"Yeah," said Jack. "I gotta agree with Amanda on this one. Gonna be tough competing with the Christmas Cave."

"I've been doing a little research." There was the hint of conspiracy in Daniel's voice. He pointed to Jack's phone. "Now me, I have a PC with a wired Internet connection."

"Ah... the web," Jack sighed. "Nice place, I hear."

Amanda pointedly ignored her brother. "Research?" she prompted.

"The Old Man. Bill's Old Man."

"How?" asked Jack.

"I looked up some of the words that Bill said the Old Man used. He was Norwegian."

"Yeah?"

"What does that give us?" asked Amanda.

"So then I looked up earthquakes in Norway over the last few weeks." He grinned then. "I think I found it. A few miles east of a town called Hamar."

"Okay, Daniel." Amanda was just a little bit impressed. "I'll bite. What are we going to do with that?"

"I'm going to go there."

"You're going to go there..."

Jack slid forward, gave a slow, knowing nod. "You're going to look for the portal the Old Man went through to reach the cave. You're going back."

"Our tunnels are done for," said Daniel. "There's no way we'll ever reach our own portal again. But the other, the Norwegian portal, might still be accessible. Each year at Christmas."

"For nine days."

"How do you know it still exists?" asked Amanda. "We didn't see it in the cave."

"We never looked for it. We know it existed once. The Old Man is proof of that."

"And the earthquakes in Norway," Jack said, nodding.

"I think it was open. This week."

"You're going back in," said Jack. "That's cool."

"Yeah."

"And just how do you plan on getting to Norway to search for the way back in?" asked Amanda.

"Obviously I'm not going now," said Daniel. "I am twelve, after all. I doubt I'd make it home before dark. But I can plan for it now. And in six years, I'm taking a trip for Christmas."

"To Norway..."

"They got reindeer there, ya' know," Daniel grinned.

"I like it," said Jack. "Yes, I do. Very much. You mind a little company?"

"I thought you'd never ask."

Daniel and Jack both turned expectantly to Amanda.

Amanda frowned, sighed. "Reindeer, huh?" She hesitated, then grumbled through a soft smile. "I'm glad you're better."

And Daniel was feeling better. Off his meds, and so far, so good. Everyone was hopeful; for Daniel and for Jenny.

Olivia called out from the living room. "Jack! Amanda! Come on out here!"

Out in the living room, the Christmas tree was glowing bright with lights, everyone was gathered 'round it. Amanda went over to her mom, who reached out and pulled her in close.

Jack watched from the hall as they all started to sing Silent Night. His grandma Jenny pulled Bill near her on one side, and Mike in close on the other.

Daniel went to his parents and Emma wrapped an arm around him. Carl rested a hand on his shoulder.

Daniel turned and looked back at Jack.
They smiled at one another.
They had plans for the future.
Norway.
And reindeer.

End

www.ingramcontent.com/pod-product-compliance
Lightning Source LLC
Chambersburg PA
CBHW051830170626
46807CB00003B/1107